Copyright ©Jodie Whiting 2023
First published 2023. Amazon kindle dire‹
Amazon.co.uk
ISBN: 9798862573909
Imprint: Independently published

Contents

Introduction

Once upon a time, there was a thirty, nearly forty something year old woman who lived with her husband and two children an ordinary life.

She had family, friends, a job, hobbies, dreams...
She had many emotions!

This is a poetry diary of the things which happened to her throughout the year. Fifty two poems, thirteen poems for each season in a poetry diary.

That's one poem for each week of the year because a poem per week helps the world seem less bleak!

Sometime in Spring

4th March, spotted some more grey hairs! They tend to catch me unawares.

Embrace the grey

Nestled in among the black,
Are the odd grey hairs which keep growing back,
Shall I dye my hair? Bleach? Remove?
I guess that Hollywood would approve.

But as they glisten in the light,
They have a beauty in their own right,
Ageing is a privilege, not a curse,
A natural process, it could be worse.

I have a healthy head of hair,
That not everyone is lucky enough to share,
So as the grey hairs can't all be kept at bay,
I think it is time to embrace the grey.

27th March, international whiskey day. Just a little drop for a night cap.

Whiskey

I can smell...floral notes of toasted vanilla, smokey new wood, berry.

I can taste...citric, nutty, leathery, leafy, sherry.

I can hear...another bottle opening, pour out the last bit but don't be too hasty.

I can see...we have drunk the lot, I guess it wassssh kwite taaaasteee.

29th March, international mermaid day. As they are fictitious, I shall cause no offense by insulting their way of life.
I must remember to bath the kids later.

Never trust a mermaid

They will lure you to the rocks,
They are not after your socks,
The sailors will meet their demise,
If by their song, you are entranced by their prize,
Never trust a mermaid.

They comb their hair with shells as a bra,
The underwater world of Atlantis think they have gone too far,
Not sure how they procreate, I am not sure if you are?
Never trust a mermaid.

They could use their powers for good if they wish,
Lure men to the rocks and feed them fresh fish,
Nurse up their wounds and send them on their way, instead of sitting on their tails all day,
They do have very luscious hair,
I guess that we will leave it there.
Never trust a mermaid.

4th April, School holidays, 1pm, Leisure centre.

Trampolining

I need to do more exercise,
I need to just relax,
I have a list of chores to do,
We're nearly out of snacks!

I need to do more exercise,
Go for a run, get some fresh air,
Hula hoop or cycle,
Feel the wind in my hair.

I need to do more exercise,
I do know my mistake,
my kids are trampolining,
I am sitting eating cake.

8th April, 2pm, Craft activity to amuse the kids.

A little bird

A little bird told me,
it's draw a picture of a bird day,
So before it flew away,
I attached an edible poem to its wing, with a little
piece of string and sent it on its way.

I would let you have a peak,
but it kept it in its beak,
and ate up the words that I quite intended to say.

11th April, is among other things, national submarine day. Let's write about that and leave the washing for a bit.

Submarine

I am immersed in your splendor,
you underwater defender,
Sub aquatic creature of the sea, submerged in
mystery.

The Beatles sang about you in yellow,
I would prefer one in sage green,
This poem is quite niche,
if you do not own a submarine.

13th April, around 1pm I saw a beautiful butterfly.
I wonder if it knows it used to be a caterpillar.

Butterfly

As I was running through the woods,
I saw a butterfly,
It fluttered its delicate colourful wings,
as it flew on by.

In that moment of serenity,
among the flowers in the wood,
The sun painted the trees with gold,
and life was sweet and good.

27th April, Email from the school, update on school dinners.

Email from the school

I am sorry to declare,
but please all be aware,
that stuffed peppers,
well they need to be replaced.

Instead the kids will find,
for their very own piece of mind,
stuffed butternut squash for them to taste.

We know it could be problematic,
so now please don't get emphatic,
the following dishes have indeed been quite
affected.

We have advised you accordingly,
there are some changes to their tea.
I need remind you,
These items will not go undetected.

It may be foolash for the goulash,
Unwise for the chicken pies,
Silly for the chilli,

A mistake for the pasta bake,
Disasterole for the casserole,
Out of control for toad in the hole,

Quite obscene for vegetable tagine,
Full of ennui for ratatouille,

Full of woe for jacket potato,
All will be rectified tomorrow.

We advise you to stop storing peppers in your houses if you please,
So we can carry on with all of our pepper related recipes.

Next week's stuffed peppers will once again be quite delicious,
But fear not...
Butternut squash is equally nutritious.

30th April, 8am. To do list: buy shop, go to milk, err hold on a minute...

To do list gone wrong

Monday:

Collect children,
unlock door with key,
throw off coats,
brew pot of tea,
chop up veggies,
soak dishes,
clean teeth,
gaze at the fishes.

Wednesday:

Unlock children,
clean door with key,
gaze at coats,
chop up pot of tea,
brew veggies,
throw dishes,
soak teeth,
collect fishes.

Friday:

Soak children,
throw door with key,

clean coats,
unlock pot of tea,
gaze at veggies,
chop up dishes,
collect teeth,
brew fishes.

6th May, soft play party 3pm.

Ball gown lady

The lady in soft play is wearing a full length
sequined gown,
I am quite sure she is the best dressed in Chatham
town.

I hope she doesn't attempt the ball pit and slide
whilst upside down.

Someone pick up that mislaid party hat and give
that lady a crown!
She supersedes the Spider-man and scary looking
clown.

15th May, 5pm, conversation with husband over how all of the spices begin with the same letter.

C Spices

All of the spices in the cupboard begin with C,
Cinnamon, cumin, coriander, chilli,
Chinese five spice,
do you see my reasoning?
Cardamom and cloves,
Cajun seasoning.

Well I hope you agree,
it's a con-spice-racy if you ask me.

Good job there is smoked paprika so it all tastes delicious,
and to make it less suspicious,
along with turmeric and saffron from Mauritius.

19th May, 4pm oranges in fruit bowl look very green.

Green oranges

"Mummy, those oranges look rather green."
"The greenest oranges I have ever seen."
"Perhaps they are mouldy or are they not ripe yet?"
"Don't worry love, you really need not fret".

"Oranges do taste best when they are orange, it's true,"
"A blueberry is best when it's purple-y blue."
"A green strawberry would not taste too good in a wine."
"A green pepper or apple? Well, that would be fine."
"Green tomatoes, they could work quite well in a chutney,"
"Bananas when green are best left on the fruit tree."

"So now we are coming to the end of this rhyme,"
"I have a tangy conclusion to this citrussy crime."
"It will in fact taste quite sublime,"
"For this green orange identifies as a lime."

30th May, watching the news, lots of strikes going on at the moment.

Strike

This poem is on strike!
It has had enough,
It demands a minimum level of wit and satire and
less of the fluff.

Sometimes these poems are too short and the pay
per word doesn't cut the mustard.
It demands days off so it doesn't get flustered.
The trains, buses and post do not run on words
alone,
This poem is the only one holding its own.

It doesn't want to schmooze you with the daft,
Silly words like bamboozle and codswallop will
not make the final draft.

What about the odes, sonnets and haiku?
It's about time someone thought all this through.
So until further notice, poetry will see no
editions…
Until I see an improvement in the working
conditions.

Sometime in Summer

4th June, national cheese day. I might fancy a bit of cheese before bed.

Say Cheese

Say cheese!
Can you be more specific?
Okay, a lovely Roquefort?
That would be terrific.

Feta make this quick,
We have not ricotta all day,
These cheese puns are worsening by the way,
How about Emmental and Gruyère?
That's just Swiss-ful thinking,
I Gouda go,
I cheddar stop, before the cheese all starts
stinking.

I hope all these cheeses are as good as they could
brie,
Take me Parmesan,
I will have some for my tea.

5th June, Global running day, went for a run.

Run, Jodie, run

I saw you running the other day,
Some of my family and friends say,
I am surprised they recognize me so disheveled
and sweaty,
Maneuvering around like an inflexible yeti.

It never gets easier running up hill,
Even though everyone insists that it will,
It seems to me, you might agree, it is all about
consistency!
Just keep on trudging along is the key,
One day it might come more easily.

Once I have run I feel elated,
Endorphins, you are appreciated,
Resist the urge to eat and drink copious amounts
of wine and cake,
Or there is no point in running for goodness
sake?!

Keep to the path, keep to the path,
Really big hill, feel my wrath!
If I could plot out all my runs on a graph,
Then my favourite run? My favourite run?
Would be the running of a bath.

20th June, school reports received from school.

Je ne sais quoi

Today I received your school reports,
I read about all the things you have done,
Of all achievements and improvements,
Of all the star pegs and dockets that you have
won.

What you cannot score on a test though,
What is impossible to convey,
Is that 'je ne sais quoi' of YOU-ness,
That comes from the beauty inside only your
DNA.

So yes, I have received your school reports,
I am so incredibly proud,
But I would like to add an addendum,
For some unknown things that need to be shouted
out loud.

No-one mentioned how you can touch your nose
with your tongue,
How your dry sense of humour keeps us all
young,
How you can wiggle your ears and talk in your
sleep,

Or how you can whistle as loud as a chimney sweep.

No-one wrote how you stroke my hair if you see I have 'tired eyes',
Or how you could recite such detailed memories as though they were televised,
How you don't miss a single word I say, even if you think it has been ignored,
How you make up songs for me whilst I shower so I 'don't get bored'.

Thank you for all the 'je ne sais quoi' moments that no-one can score,
I look forward to a lifetime of so many more.

25th June, 8pm. A fox stole my sandal. He is yet to return it.

Oh Fox

Oh fox, oh fox, with your auburn hair,
There is something you should know as you head to your lair,
When you forage for treasure, could you leave my new shoes there?
For I really prefer my new shoes as a pair.

I know the smell of leather is what you desire,
I did not foresee what would transpire,
I am not sure the sandal will suit your attire,
It is really not an item you need to require.

Oh fox, oh fox, if it's alright with you,
The sandal which you decided to chew,
The one which I bought which was shiny and new.
I will exchange for an old, ropy one. Can we please talk this through?

Oh fox, oh fox, with your auburn hair,
I know you cannot read this and really do not care,
But for next time in case you catch me unaware…
I really prefer my new shoes as a pair.

2nd July, house is quiet and the kids are playing nicely…

Mischief

My kids are not up to mischief, is this trickery?
They are helping me make dinner,
harmoniously…

I am under no illusion,
I have reached just one conclusion.

No-one is shouting, no-one is weeping,
Someone must have swapped my kids whilst I
was sleeping.

They look the same, I can't see any gears,
I am looking for wires behind their ears,
Oh no, wait, they have resorted to default fight
mode,
Can someone re-programme the restore calm
code?

I believe these kids are indeed worth keeping,
So please don't replace these ones whilst I am
sleeping.

10ᵗʰ July, so many things to do, so little time…

Time

Can somebody please find a way,
To stop time for a few hours per day?
So I can enjoy the smell of the flowers,
Ponder and procrastinate for hours,
Without it affecting the days plans in motion,
Now wouldn't that be quite the notion.

A halt on time to write this rhyme.

....
....

Okay, I am not sure it worked?
The sandman is calling me in for a meeting,
Better dash as time is fleeting.

I met a time traveller in my dreams,
He said to stop being frivolous, time is just as it
seems.
I tried to trade secrets with an old time monger,
But turns out, I am not getting any younger.

22ⁿᵈ July, Summer holidays, kids need more snacks. How many weeks are left?

Hungry

On Monday, my children ate through one apple,
but they were still hungry it seemed,
On Tuesday, my children ate through two pears,
poached, not steamed,
On Wednesday, my children ate through three
plums, but it was not enough to fill their tums,
On Thursday, four strawberries, you would think
they would be pleased!
On Friday, five oranges, "but we're still hungry"
they cried, so more food I supplied.

On Saturday, they ate through cakes and on the
sly, they guzzled through some cherry pie, a
watermelon slice was rather nice, cones of ice
cream was quite the dream, not forgetting
lollipops and charcuterie, all washed down with
sausage and pickle for tea.

Then on Sunday, they ate through one green leaf,
and they felt much better to my relief.

Now I realise this is all too familiar, turns out it
was all the hungry caterpillar.
"Mummy, that's plagiarism," they probably said.
Let's finish this story and head off to bed.

28th July, My daughter got back on her bike after a year and her determination inspires me.

Believe in yourself

Layla stood by her bike for the first time in one year,
She had forgotten how to ride, but she had no fear.

"I believe in myself, I am Layla Faye and I will ride my bike today."
She fell a few times, but that is okay,
"I believe in myself, I am Layla Faye and I will ride my bike today."

She rode her bike and emerged victorious,
With the wind in her hair and her hair wild and glorious.

Believe in yourself, don't over complicate,
Do not over think it, do not sit and wait.

Believe in yourself, Layla knew that she could,
And I of course,
well,
I knew that she would.

4th August, my daughter is testing my patience midway through holidays.

Little darlings

My daughter can be very charming,
Kind and considerate, happy and calming,
But right now she is flying in to a rage,
Somebody go and waft around sage.

Calm is required and where is the wine?
Normally, she behaves just fine.

For apart from when she is 'misunderstood',
We all love her dearly and all is good.

Hormones can be tricky when our darlings are growing,
But it's just a phase, so where is this going?

When she is older, she will be my saviour,
Teenagers are well known for their rational behaviour.

For apart from when she is 'misunderstood',
We all love her dearly and all is good.

If all else fails and to stop me from weeping,
She really is a darling when she is sleeping.

13th August, Left handers day. The struggle is real…

Left handers are right

In the olden days, for being left-handed,
You would have been reprimanded!
She is such a 'leftie', more left-handed than some
other left handers they say,
In the office, I would even file left handed,
putting everything away, to their dismay.
'We know you have been here, it's all the wrong
way', they would say.

Luckily now I can hide it you see,
Everything is filed electronically,
I laugh with glee.

At school, they would pass me the rounders bat,
Oh wait, she is left handed, she will need a few
minutes to compensate for that.

Don't get me started on left handed scissors
please,
I use right handed scissors confidently, with ease!

How do you use a potato peeler?
Same way as you, I suppose?

I can eat right handed and I have the correct
number of toes.
It's probably just her personality, for which I am
synonymous,
I am off to join left handers anonymous.

19th August, potato day. Which one shall I cook tonight?

Potato

Oh potato, potato,
I hope that you know,
I will butter you up,
Because I love you so.

I yam in awe of your greatness,
From the ground you have spurted,
So let's not hesistater,
I am potatolly converted,
Our friendchip is strong,
Carb haters gonna hate,
But their chip has sailed,
We all know you taste great.

22nd August, two kids, two strong personalities, can they agree?

Agree

"I want ham!"
"I want cheese!"
Well, first of all, it's 'Can I please?'
Let me put my mind at ease.

I will make your sandwiches as you so desire them to be,
It would all be so much easier if you two could just agree.

"I want to go out!"
"I want to go fast!"
"I want to play football."
"I want to go last."

Well, first of all, it's 'Can I please?'
Can we compromise and hear my plea?
It would all be so much easier if you two could just agree.

Imagine having three...

30th August, one of the perks of being a mum is how much your kids appreciate you…

Sweet wrapper

"I am stuck on a desert island, the pirates have stranded me ashore,"
Excuses my child has given me to not help with a chore.

"I am too tired, I am too cold, I'm playing Lego on the floor,"
Excuses my child has given me to not help with a chore,
"I do everything around this place, I cannot possibly do more!"
Excuses my child has given me to not help with a chore.

"You're right, all I have done is…
Physically, mentally and emotionally dedicated my life to you on cue, picking up your sweet wrapper from the floor was too much to ask of you…"

Sometime in Autumn

2nd September, I wonder what the worst job would be. I certainly don't envy this one.

I would rather

I would rather be groom of the stool for the king,
Watch that programme on telly where no-one can sing,
Be ball picker-upper in the kids' soft play,
Scoop up prison gloop from a prisoner's tray,
Than be prime minister for the day.

I would rather be a poverty stricken character from Dickens,
Re-chew the food from an old brood of chickens,
Give the kiss of life to an MP than to say,
That I was prime minister for the day.

I would rather be swallowed whole by a whale,
And live to tell the sorry tale,
Drink a poisonous, revolting potion,
Than be prime minister in all this commotion.

I would rather slump in to a wheelie bin,
Live my life without coffee and gin,
Than be the one leading the track,
In the game of prime minister-hit the road Jack.

Where was I?

I should really hang out the washing in the sun,
I could arrange in colour order just for fun.

As I was saying, today is national…

I might make a fancy French cake with crème patisserie,
Maybe not, I will just watch cake programmes on TV.

So today, 6th September is national procrastination day!

My fringe could do with a trim,
Now where was I? How to write a good poem.

I guess I should get this poem redacted,
As I am very easily distracted.

8th September, Pirate day at school.

Rrrr me hearties

It's pirate day at school today,
So with a shiver me timbers in the air,
We headed out, no messing about,
With a squawk and an ahoy there!

The menu was ladened with pirate puns,
Treasure trove baked beans, they scream,
Walk the plank was to be frank,
Ill partnered with lemon ice cream.

On its own without these words,
The kids might be ignoring,
But how can Captain Jack chicken, pirates a
trickin',
Swashbuckling potatoes be boring?

They couldn't dress up, but they were provided,
with a pencil and a hat,
So art could be drawn instead of swords,
I could hardly complain about that.

Dressed in black for the occasion,
Layla found a black coat that 'wowed',
As uniform states black coat and tights, they are
allowed.

Now most teachers with thirty kids would not notice or even stop,
But straight away the teacher spotted the case of the coat swap.

"Layla!" she exclaimed with a massive grin,
"Well come aboard the boat!"
"For what we have here, now give a big cheer,"
"Is an 'Rrrrr' kind of coat!"

So Layla's teacher, Mrs T,
She really is the bees knees!
We danced together a jig, for I don't give a fig,
More 'Rrrrr' me hearties if you please!

14th September. Wedding anniversary. Husband and I have a conversation which goes something like this:
me: "Why do we need to go to the beach so early?
Husband: "I cannot control the tides."
We laughed for a while.

The tides

I love my husband very much,
He makes me laugh and smile and such,
"The only thing is," he confides,
"I am afraid I cannot control the tides."

He tried to control them the other day,
The waves and sea monsters got in the way,
I have decided to love him in spite of this
confession,
I will allow this small transgression.

So as long as he can control the sun and the
transience of life,
I will continue to be his wife.

28th September, around 4pm, discover mystery sock on floor…

Abandoned sock

Lying on the bathroom floor,
Smelly and unclean,
That one small sock which missed the wash,
It did not make it to the machine.

It came out of the laundry basket,
Then danced its way across the floor,
The small sock owner was distracted,
She did not want that sock anymore.

The Lycra bib shorts, they all made it,
So did the uniform for school,
But as for that poor, abandoned sock,
Life can be so cruel.

Friday 13th October, superstitions are rife!
Perhaps I should stay in bed.

Superstitions

It's Friday the 13th, my friends,
So paint those black cats white,
Transport those mirrors with great care,
Unless you want a fright.

Remove all ladders from applicable occupations,
Well I know that you might scoff,
But it's probably for the best, window cleaners,
If you all take the day off.

Don't touch noses to avoid those itches,
Keep those new shoes well away from the table,
Don't kiss across thresholds (or any kind of
holds!)
And knock on wood if you are able.

For those worth their salt, don't throw over
shoulders.
Don't open umbrellas inside,
If bad luck comes in threes, then lose count if you
please,
And never cross knives, unless you have already
tried.

Salute all those magpies,
And if all else fails and you are not thinking
clearly,
Ignore all these things,
Well, it's all nonsense really!

I am off to step on a manhole,
Or gender neutral one if unsure,
If I make it home alive, without a scrape of
demise,
Please put my rabbit's foot by the door.

16th October, weekly shop. Meet husband at supermarket.

Shopping date

We used to have our dates in exotic places,
Cinema, restaurants, a day at the races,
But tonight I will meet you, don't be late,
It's time for the weekly shop shopping date!

I'll meet you at the freezer full of ice creams,
We'll gaze at each other over the aisle of dreams,
We'll compare the price of the own brand
wheetabix,
This probably won't get its own show on Netflix.

We have picked up some bargains,
Clean up on aisle three!
Let's load up the boot,
And have a nice cup of tea.

19th October, in the café.

Conversations overheard

"They put a flame in your ear for your ear wax,"
"I wouldn't mind having a go,"
"I couldn't tell him his suit didn't suit him,"
"I am not sure they care at a funeral though,"
"I'm sorry we are out of the pumpkin spiced
latte,"
Conversations overheard whilst sitting in the
café.

"The large is too large, but with the small I took
one sip!"
"Usher her over, she is after a tip,"
"She fell over in the launderette, she's done
something to her hip,"
"Therapy is better than counselling they say,"
Conversations overheard whilst sitting in the
café.

I don't know who these strangers are,
Snippets taken out of context,
I only caught a few lines, I do not know what
happened next,
I have finished off my coffee, "Thank you, come
again one day,"
Conversations overheard whilst sitting in the
café.

31st October, Halloween, parent's evening, school disco, list of things in my brain…

List

Parent's evening, Halloween,
Costumes looking all pristine,
School disco, don't forget the ticket,
Put it in an envelope, lick it, stick it,
Catch the bus to work again,
This is a list of the things in my brain.

Dinner, run the kids their baths,
Teach the youngest about split digraphs,
Dance in the kitchen just for laughs,
Cup of tea, washing up is piling,
Read to the kids and keep on smiling,
Snuggle up in a blanket, put the kids to bed,
This is a list of the things in my head.

Run up a hill and try to talk,
Next time I am going to walk,
Have we run out of washing up liquid?
Why can't I ever find a Tupperware lid?
Remember the name of the birthday kid,
I think that it is going to rain,
This is a list of the things in my brain.

Who went out of the dancing last night?

Who do you think would win in a fight: a
vampire bat or a common mole?

Concentrate on the casserole,
Put the leftovers in a bowl,
Wash up, hoover, clean and sweep,
This is a…
Brain, please go to sleep.

8ᵗʰ November, colds are doing the rounds again.
Snotty children, lack of sleep zzzz.

Case of the colds

I am down in the dumps,
with a bang and some bumps,
I am a gloomy old camel with too many humps.

My plans have changed, I will suck and brood,
I am in a not so happy, snappy, kind of mood.

My kid is magnetized to me full of cold, snot and
drool,
Off sick and not able to go to school.

She will perk up later, calpol will do the trick,
Someone pass me my other kid quick- he is not
yet sick.

Tomorrow is another day as they say,
Hopefully it is not full of cold or dismay.

16th November, my daughter asked me why
unicorns are not real. There is no logical answer.

No sense for unicorns

A koala's brain is smooth,
It has no lumps or bumps,
Narwhals, they have a massive tusk,
Camels, they have humps.

Rhinos, they can weight three tonnes,
Jellyfish can sting,
But wait, I don't, it doesn't...why aren't unicorns
a thing?

So when my young daughter questions this,
And makes a wish for me,
To own a real life unicorn,
Well, please can we agree.

There is no sense or logic,
So how can I explain?
How unicorns are nonsense,
But dinosaurs ruled this plain?

20th November, cleaning bathroom, counting the toothbrushes...

Eleven toothbrushes

We had eleven toothbrushes in our bathroom,
Four, five or six would suffice,
I am not sure how they got there,
But I counted them, thrice!

I really feel I don't have too many excuses,
Brushing four sets of teeth are their only real uses.
Except for cleaning all the bike chains,
Or for scrubbing out some old clothes stains.

I threw away the ropier ones,
They can't be recycled you see,
I am off to write,
Some more interesting poetry.

27th November, making sandwiches, Finley alarmingly informs me there is no tomato in his sandwich.

There is no tomato in my sandwich

"I have a pocket full of sand,"
"A gem stone and a rock."
"Some Pokémon cards,"
"A piece of Lego and a sock."

"I have a drawing of a plane,"
"A rubber and some glue."
"A tiny little dinosaur,"
"And a blanket which is blue."

"But what I don't have is round, it is squishy and bright red,"
"I don't have a tomato in my sandwich," Finley said.

"I have a heart full of love,
"A room full of toys,"
"Some camouflage attire like some other little boys."
"I have an iPad which is purple,"
"Cuddly toys on my bed".
"A list of many questions, both written down and in my head."
"But what I don't have is a fruit, but it is a vegetable, there's no doubt,"

"A tomato in my sandwich, that's the thing I am without."

"I have bacon flavoured crisps."
"Some ham if you please."
"A bread fort to contain them,"
"And in between you'll find some cheese,"

"I have butter, I hear you utter,"
"But now please don't be misled…"
"There is no tomato in my sandwich," Finley said.

Sometime in Winter

1ˢᵗ December, snowing, ice, hills... not a great mix.

Slipping

I am slipping down a massive mug of tea,
Slipping in to a thermal vest and all of the comfy,
I am slipping under these festive piles of
wrapping paper, one, two and three,
I am slipping into a Christmas coma of mince pies
and stollen, can anyone see me?

I
AM
  SLIIIII
    IIPING
      DOOOOOOWN
        THIS
         HILL.

Help me!

I prefer my ice in a G&T.

8th December, observations on the bus. I may never see that lady again.

The lady on the bus

The lady on the bus has ringlets in her hair,
And huge gold earrings of varying sizes hanging
from her ears,
I did not mean to stare!

Five lots of rings in rose gold,
It is a sight to behold!
I am both bedazzled and befuddled by her array
of ringlets and rings,
The bus stops; I move on to other things.

15ᵗʰ December, supermarket confusion.
Misunderstandings in the aisle.

The man

I thought I heard the man in the supermarket talk
to me,
What he said though was a bit of a mystery,
I could ponder a while over it,
It didn't make much sense you see.

He told me not to forget the stakes,
When were the stakes high?
I wonder what I had done to lose everything so
carelessly?

Have I lived a life of regret, full of unexpected
melancholy?

"Do you want them love?"
Oh, the steaks... silly me.

27th December, that period between Christmas and new year where no-one knows what is going on or what day it is, or how much cheese they have eaten.

Mystery diet

I haven't lost any weight,
It is a puzzle I am sure,
All I have done is changed nothing,
I hope there is a cure.

I've weighed out my porridge, two bowls for me.
Eaten some lettuce leaves, soaked in wine, meat and brie,
It's a real mystery.

I have done lots of walking, to the fridge and the bath,
Ate a large box of chocolates,
But consumed only half.

I ran thirty miles in my dreams,
But my watch was switched off,
I ate a carrot and a cracker,
With the takeaway I did scoff.

And if I stare really hard at the diet book,
At the lady who has that toned and tanned look,
I start to look more like her than I thought,
Though that could be down to the bottle of port.

2nd January, too much alcohol and a cold equals a lot of snoring for the husband to put up with.

Snore

I will listen to your woes and share out each chore,
I will share your umbrella if the rains does pour,
I will present you with your dinner when you get through the door,
If you could please put up with me when I snore.

I will be your financial guarantor,
I will remove your dirty socks from the floor,
I will share the last piece of my chocolate, isn't that what love's for?
If you could please put up with me when I snore.

I will tidy away all of your things in a drawer,
Understand your love of bikes and the need to have more,
I think that we now know the score,
I will do many things for the sake of 'amour',
If you can please put up with me when I snore.

5th January, I have the lurgy. A friend gave my this advice.

Rest up well

Stay well rested and fed,
In your cosy, little bed,
Just keep warm and watered,
Don't do too much if you can't.

Keep directly out of sunlight,
Oh no, wait, that advice,
That advice...
It was meant for a plant.

*10th January, enjoying my new present. I may
never leave the house again.*

New blanket

I have a new item of clothing,
It is navy, comfy and clean,
It is the cosiest, softest, most velvet-est, wearable
blanket I have ever seen.

It is smooth like a silky, hot chocolate,
It is fluffy and floats on air,
It has pockets and flatters at every angle,
I am without a whisper of a care.

The trouble is now I have it on,
It is quite possible, it's true,
That I may never take it off,
My fantastic gown of blue.

If you see a hibernating cuddly creature,
Snuggling down with a big cup of tea,
Well, don't be alarmed,
I mean you no harm.
It is the lesser known pyjama shaped me.

18th January, caterpillar related emergency. There isn't a special hot-line for caterpillar emergencies, which is weird when you think about it...

Caterpillar emergency

When your kids tell you to come as quickly as you can,
And you run to the scene of the crime, that's the plan.
It turns out an emergency just isn't the same,
When you're a child and learning the rules of life game.

A caterpillar is on the floor and it might be a threat?
It seems we have found ourselves a harmless, new pet,
The next time your kid shouts,
It's probably a false alarm.
Just a lump of cheese in the corner,
So please remain calm.

25th January. Daughter loses coat in playground and it is gone forever, apparently?

Coat confusion

My child, she lost her coat one day,
She left it on the playground bench during play,
The teachers said it was quite the surprise,
It disappeared before their eyes.

They checked the bins and usual places,
Confusion planted upon their faces.

"We have never had this happen before," the teachers, they did say,
My daughter's explanation was that it simply blew away.

Drifted off in the wind, to a faraway land, to wherever it wanted to go,
We never saw that coat again,
I guess we'll never know.

I hope it is happy, nice and warm,
Wherever it might be,
If you see a pink coat floating off in the wind,
Will you kindly catch it for me?

1ˢᵗ February, dropped the blueberries all over the kitchen. It's one of those days. Ahhhhhh!

Everything is fine

I've dropped the blueberries everywhere!
Everything is fine,
I can't find any clean underwear,
Everything is fine.

The kids are arguing, distracting me,
Everything is fine,
I need to get on with cooking the tea,
Everything is fine.

The house is a mess and I am tired,
Everything is fine,
I don't have the email password required,
EVERYTHING IS FINE!

Everything is…
Everything is in a bit of a muddle,
I think I really need a cuddle.

5th February, daughter won't eat her dinner up nicely and it is stressful.

An unrelaxing mealtime

My daughter won't eat her dinner,
She is annoyed and has her reasons,
She will not be persuaded,
We will be here for all the seasons.

I would like to enjoy my strogonoff,
Tell my daughter to buzz off,
She may shout and she may hiss,
I no longer wish to entertain this.

If I could stay calm, we must stay calm,
Try to ignore that she is poking my arm,
Try to stay ahhhhhhhlarmingly zen..
She eats just the rice,
We'll call it a day then.

14th February, Valentine's day. I shouldn't care about love day, but I secretly wish to be showered with roses and chocolates.

Valentine's day nonsense

We know it's consumerism, not really love day,
Capitalist society, the price that we pay.

But if you don't receive a card,
You can't help feeling blue,
Even though it's all nonsense and the rational
you…

Says you don't need flowers or a box full of
hearts,
Or strawberries and cream over bodily parts.

"We're too old for that," my husband said,
"I could send you a note saying I love you
instead."

"Okay," I say, "Instead of a card on this day,
You can write me a note with something different
to say,
Fifty two days rather than one,
If this is the option you choose just for fun."

"If you write fifty two notes full of love that's sincere,
Instead of a card on one day of the year,
If you write me a note every day and don't stop…"

"On seconds thoughts" he said,
"I think I'll pop to the shop."

28th February, husband brings me a cup of tea,
like he does every morning. So this is a fitting
poem to end my diary.

Love

You bring my morning cup of tea,
"Thank you," I say. "This pleases me."

Later on we watch the telly or listen to our
favourite podcast.
You throw your smelly socks on the floor.
And they say love doesn't last?!

You acknowledge my existence,
We have a wine or beer.
I look at you, it makes me smile.
I love you, I'm glad you are here.

Acknowledgements

I would like to thank my two children Finley Whiting and Layla Whiting for providing a lot of the content for my diary. I love you both very much.

To my husband Matthew Whiting for his love, support and morning cups of tea.

To my mum Kim Hill, who inspires me every day and nurtures and supports me always.
To my step dad Richard Hill for his love, support and proof reading skills.
To my sister Carly Harris and my brother Thomas Faber for their love, support and guidance.

To all my amazing family, with special thanks, in alphabetical order to: Sarah Faber, Anna Field, David Field, David Harris, Julie Smith, Robert Smith, Jane Whiting and Stephen Whiting.

To my friends and colleagues and anyone who has ever liked or commented on my poems, with particular thanks to Katie Mash for her help in creating a website for my poems.

To loved ones lost and remembered, with a special mention to Barbara Allen.

I dedicate this book to my Nan and Grandad June Doreen Williams and Henry Thomas Williams, who always had such love and pride for their children, grandchildren and great grandchildren. You are forever in our hearts.

Index of poems

Printed in Great Britain
by Amazon